Outside My Window

LIESEL MOAK SKORPEN
PICTURES BY
MERCER MAYER

HARPERCOLLINS*PUBLISHERS*

Manufactured in China by South China Printing Company Ltd.
All rights reserved.
www.harperchildrens.com

Library of Congress Cataloging-in-Publication Data
Skorpen, Liesel Moak.
  Outside my window / by Liesel Moak Skorpen ; pictures by Mercer Mayer.
    p.   cm.
  Summary: No matter what the little boy does to disguise the small bear he
finds looking in his bedroom window one night, it still looks like a bear, and
must be returned to its mother bear in the forest.
  ISBN 0-06-050774-8 — ISBN 0-06-050775-6 (lib. bdg.)
  [1. Bears—Fiction.] I. Title.

PZ7.S62837 Ou 2004
[Fic]

1 2 3 4 5 6 7 8 9 10
❖

For Jana Marie Skorpen, Richard (Rye) Whitney Tifft III,
Miles Nathaniel Skorpen, and Tess Elizabeth Tifft
—L.M.S.

To Diane Dubreuil
—M.M.

A little boy was going to bed.
He looked out the window and saw there,
looking at him, a small bear.

His mother was in the kitchen.

"Mother," he said,
"there's a bear outside my window.
He's looking in at me."

"It's time for bed," his mother said.

His father was in the sitting room.

"Father," he said,
"outside my window there's a bear.
He's looking in at me."

"It's time for bed," his father said.

So the little boy went back into his room.
He looked out his window.
A small bear with sad eyes was looking in.

"Good-night, bear," said the little boy softly.
He climbed into bed and turned out the light.

He couldn't sleep.
He heard his sister going to bed.
He heard his mother and his father going to bed.
Still he couldn't sleep.
So he climbed out of bed.
He found his flashlight,
and he shined it out the window.

And there was the small bear with eyes so sad
that the little boy opened the window wide
and let the bear come in.

"Are you lost?" he asked.

The bear didn't say anything.
He just sat there looking lost.

"Please don't cry," said the little boy.
He had a few pieces of candy left from Halloween.

He found them and gave them to the bear.
And the bear ate them,
paper and all, and licked his paws.

"Bear," said the little boy, "I like you.
I'd like to keep you here with me.
I'd ask my mother,
but you know how mothers are.
If only you weren't so like a bear.
If only you were a sort of furry dog."

The boy had an old dog's collar in his drawer,
so he tried that on the bear.
Then he showed the bear how dogs sit,
and he put a rubber ball in his mouth.

But the bear didn't look
like a furry dog.
He looked like a bear
with a ball in his mouth.

"Never mind," said the little boy,
"I've another idea.
My mother doesn't care for bears,
but she is very fond of little boys."

He found some pants and his Sunday shirt,
and some socks and some shoes
which weren't a good fit.
The bear tried to help with the buttons,
but bears aren't clever with buttons.

The little boy looked at the bear
from one side and another.
But from every side it was pretty much the same.
The bear didn't look like a little boy.
He looked like a bear with trousers on.
The bear looked at himself in the mirror.
His eyes filled up with tears.

"Please don't cry," said the little boy.
"Please don't give up yet."

He put the bear into bed
and tried to hide him there.
But the lumps and bumps
he made under the sheet
looked very like a bear in the bed.

So the little boy went down the hall
and found some of his sister's clothes.

"When you smile,"
he said to the bear hopefully,
"you look like my sister—a little at least.
And if you stayed in the shadows
and out from under foot,
perhaps my mother wouldn't notice you."

But even in a flowered hat
that bear looked like a bear.

"It's just no use," said the little boy.
"You'll have to go.
If my mother and father find you here,
they'll surely send you to the zoo."

The boy found a knitted cap in his drawer
and a warm woolen muffler.
In the kitchen he found bread and jam
and some oatmeal cookies,
and he put them in a paper sack.

The little boy put on his bathrobe and his slippers
and opened the window and out they went.
Hand in paw they crossed the garden
to the meadow's edge.
The boy gave his flashlight to the bear.

"Good-bye, bear," he said.
"Take care of yourself.
Watch out for hunters and forest fires."

And the little boy went back into the house.

He stood by the window
and watched the bear slowly cross
the meadow and climb the hill.

As the small bear reached the forest's edge
a large bear came out of the thicket.
The small bear ran to meet her,
and she took him in her arms.

"Good-bye, bear," said the little boy
as he climbed into bed and turned out the light.
"Watch out for hunters and forest fires."

After a while the little boy fell asleep.